SHOCKING SHOOTING!

AND OTHER STORIES:

FEARSOME FREE KICKS
WICKED WINGERS

MICHAEL COLEMAN
ILLUSTRATED BY NICK ABADZIS

ORCHARD BOO

Visit Michael Coleman's website!
www.michael-coleman.com

Look out for the other Angels FC books:

SQUABBLING SQUADS
DAZZLING DRIBBLING
TOUCHLINE TERROR
AWESOME ATTACKING

ORCHARD BOOKS
338 Euston Road, London NW1 3BH
Orchard Books Australia
Level 17/205 Kent St, Sydney, NSW 2000

First published in Great Britain as individual volumes
First published in Great Britain in bind-up format 2004
This edition published 2008
Shocking Shooting
Text © Michael Coleman 2000, inside illustations © Nick Abadzis 2000
Fearsome Free Kicks
Text © Michael Coleman 1999, inside illustrations © Nick Abadzis 1999
Wicked Wingers
Text © Michael Coleman 2000, inside illustrations © Nick Abadzis 2000

The rights of Michael Coleman to be identified as the author
and of Nick Abadzis to be identified as the illustrator of this work
have been asserted by them in accordance with the
Copyright, Designs and Patents Act, 1988.
A CIP catalogue record for this book is available
from the British Library.

ISBN 978 1 40830 012 1

3 5 7 9 10 8 6 4 2
Printed in Great Britain by
CPI Cox & Wyman, Reading, RG1 8EX

Orchard Books is a division of Hachette Children's Books
an Hachette UK company.
www.hachette.co.uk

A HILARIOUS HAT TRICK OF STORIES!

ANGELS FC!

Goalkeeper

Left Full Back

Right Full Back

Midfield (Centre)

Centre Back

Striker

Coa

Kirsten Browne

Barry 'Bazza' Watts

Tarlock Bhasin

Lennie Gould (Captain)

Daisy Higgins

Colin 'Co Flower

SHOCKING SHOOTING

CONTENTS

1

Kick-off!

Rhoda O'Neill shot out of the newsagents, raced all the way home, bounded up the stairs, charged into her bedroom, slammed the door shut, then dived full-length on to her bed like a goalie making a flying save.

Was it there? Was it?

Quickly she flipped through the pages of *Kick-Off!*, the glossy football magazine she bought faithfully every week.

Past the star interview page she went, past the action shots from all the top

matches, past the pull-out pin-up posters... to
the readers' letters page.

It was there! Her letter was
actually, unbelievably there!

Dear Kick-Off! magazine,
    I love playing for my
team Angels FC, but my real
ambition is to be a football kit
model like those in your advertisements.
Can you please give me some advice
on how to get started?
    Yours hopefully,
    Rhoda O'Neill (Miss)

Rhoda could hardly bear to look at
the answer. Would it encourage her? Or
would it tell her to stick to playing and
forget all about modelling because that
was a completely daft idea?

Taking a deep breath to calm herself down, Rhoda read the reply beneath her letter.

Dear Rhoda,

Everybody should have an ambition!

Good luck with yours!

The best way to get started in modelling is to build up what's called a portfolio. That's a file of photographs of yourself – perhaps even a video! Once you've got your portfolio you can send it anywhere. We'd love to see it!

Yours footballingly,

Kick-Off!

A portfolio! What a brilliant idea!

Rhoda lay back and gazed dreamily at the ceiling. She could see herself now, posing before a battery of photographers in a brand new England Women's team kit.

The kit would be as bright as her smile, not a speck of mud in sight. Now that *would* be a dream! thought Rhoda. With her all-action style she usually finished an Angels match covered in mud!

Yes, decided Rhoda, she would get a portfolio together. It should be easy. Lots of the Angels players had cameras. They'd all take pictures for her...

Rhoda had second thoughts. What if she came out looking awful? What if all the Angels laughed and said the only modelling job she'd ever get would be for Hallowe'en masks?

No, asking one of her Angels team-mates to take her picture was too risky. What she needed was a way of building up her portfolio...but *in secret!*

Sunday evening was St Jude's Youth Club night, the time when the Angels FC team forgot about playing football and came together to try other things – like watching football videos and arguing about football!

It was also the time when their coach, Trevor Rowe, known as Trev the Rev because he was also vicar of St Jude's Church, would announce any news items they needed to know about.

Hurrying through the doors, Rhoda saw that she was the last to arrive. The other players were already there and Trev was calling for some hush. Beside him stood a gangly youth whom Rhoda was sure she'd seen somewhere before.

"For those of you who don't know him," called Trev, as if reading Rhoda's mind, "let me introduce Byron Higgins. Byron is Daisy's brother."

Of course! realised Rhoda. Byron had come along to watch their games before now.

Occasionally, she now remembered, he would bring along his camera and take action pictures.

His camera? Byron was a photographer? Rhoda's mind began turning like a racing car's wheels – especially when Trev made his announcement.

"Byron has been given a project to do as part of his course at college." He turned to Daisy's brother. "Would you like to tell them about it?"

"Er...right," said Byron.

He coughed a bit, shuffled a bit, and then finally worked out what to say. "I've got to come up with an advertisement for something."

Lennie Gould, the Angels captain, thrust his hand up. "So that's why you want us to help. The Angels are an advertisement for good football, aren't they, Trev!"

"You are when you remember the Angels code," smiled Trev.

"Angels on and off the pitch!" chanted almost the whole team together. Only Rhoda's mind was elsewhere. She thrust her hand up.

"What sort of advertisement?" she asked Byron.

"Ah," said Byron, "I haven't quite worked that out yet. I'm hoping I'll get some ideas when I do my first bit of filming."  And, to Rhoda's absolute delight, he gingerly lifted a camcorder encased in bubble-wrap from his bag. "It's got to be an advert on video, see?"

An advert? A video advert? Featuring footballers? This was a way Rhoda could get her picture taken without the Angels knowing. All she would have to do then would be to get a copy of the tape and send it away to *Kick-Off!* magazine. Rhoda was ready to explode with joy. Before she knew it she'd screeched, "Brilliant!"

Everybody turned to look at her. Rhoda
flushed bright red.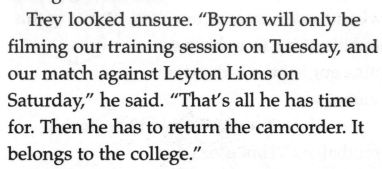
"Er...because, er...you
could use it as a training
video, couldn't you,
Trev? You know, point
out where we'd gone
wrong and all that."

Trev looked unsure. "Byron will only be
filming our training session on Tuesday, and
our match against Leyton Lions on
Saturday," he said. "That's all he has time
for. Then he has to return the camcorder. It
belongs to the college."

"So you've only got it for a week?" Rhoda
 asked Byron, wanting
to make sure
she'd understood
the position.
Byron nodded
vigorously.

"I don't *want* it longer than that! It's worth a fortune! I'm terrified of busting it!"

Rhoda did the calculations. Two filming sessions meant not much more than two hours of recording. No room for error, then. At training on Tuesday, and at the match on Saturday, she had to be looking her best!

Above all she had to ensure that, whenever Byron was recording, there in the middle of his lens was a glamorous, stunning, potential model.

Her!

2

Pass, Don't Pose!

On Tuesday afternoon Rhoda shot out of
school, raced all the way home, bounded up
the stairs, charged into her bedroom,
slammed the door shut...and spent the next
two hours getting changed for the Angels
training session.

She'd decided to get ready at home
because the changing rooms sometimes had
lumps of mud on the floor or benches, and
Rhoda didn't want the slightest speck
spoiling her appearance – not after the time

she'd spent washing and ironing her Angels shirt, pressing her shorts so that they had creases as sharp as knives and flattening her socks until they were silky smooth! She'd even washed and ironed the laces for her boots!

Finally, Rhoda set off to walk to training. What with avoiding trees in case a dirty leaf fell on her and waiting ten minutes for a muddy-pawed dog on her route to be called indoors, by the time she arrived the session was already under way.

The other players were warming up. Rhoda was about to run across and join them when she heard Trev yell, "Ten press-ups!"

Normally Rhoda wouldn't have thought twice about flinging herself on the filthy ground – but not today! She'd never yet seen a model in *Kick-Off!* magazine looking as though they'd actually played a game!

So, while the others practised sliding tackles and diving headers, Rhoda tucked herself behind a tree and watched. Finally she heard Trev call, "Practice match, everybody!" Only then did Rhoda run elegantly across to the pitch and take her place beside Lennie Gould in the line-up.

"Where have you been?" demanded Lennie.

"Having a make-over by the look of it," laughed Daisy Higgins, noting Rhoda's perfect appearance. "This is a practice match, y'know, not a fashion parade!"

Rhoda ignored them. Out on the touchline she could see Byron getting into position with his camcorder. Her video portfolio was about to get under way!

Trev blew his whistle. Jonjo Rix kicked off for Rhoda's team, rolling the ball gently sideways to Colly Flower. Colly laid it back to Lennie Gould.

Rhoda glanced out towards the touchline. The little red light at the front of Byron's camcorder had flicked on. He was recording!

"My ball, Lennie!" screamed Rhoda, zipping across in a blur of movement and shoving Lennie to one side.

Then, ignoring calls to pass the ball, she
began dribbling across the pitch until she
was right in front of Byron. There she
stopped, put her foot on the ball, and
smiled. A perfect shot for a
football kit advert!
"Should I turn round to
the left, Byron?" she
asked. "Or is my best
side on the right?"
"You can turn right
round and go home if you
like!" bawled Daisy Higgins.
"Get on with the game!"
Swivelling gracefully,
Rhoda shaped to play a long
through ball for Jonjo. But then she thought,
what if Byron decides to make an advert for
football boots rather than kit? So, instead of
passing, she lifted an elegant leg and
twiddled her ankle attractively.

Rhoda was still twiddling as Mick Ryall, playing on the other side, zoomed in to take the ball away. Seconds later he'd dribbled round Daisy and whacked the ball into the net to put Rhoda's team 0–1 down! Daisy and Lennie converged on Rhoda.

"I think Byron is looking for some action shots," snarled Daisy.

"So let's see some action," growled Lennie. "Or else!"

Action? thought Rhoda. Good idea. Maybe Byron will decide on an advert for an energy drink. In that case he'll want film of a finely-tuned athlete, racing through on goal with the ball at her feet. She looked across to see that Byron was moving to a spot beside the goal Rhoda's team were kicking into. Right, action it was!

Her chance came almost at once. Lennie won the ball in midfield. Seeing a gap ahead, Daisy powered through from behind and called for a pass. But Rhoda had other ideas. Nipping the ball off Lennie's toes, she raced through herself.

"Rhoda! Pass!" screamed Daisy, who'd carried on running.

Rhoda ignored her. For, behind the goal, she could see Byron's camcorder aimed straight at her. It was the perfect photo opportunity! She charged on, with Daisy still screaming for a pass every step of the way, until she reached the penalty area and the moment when she must surely be slap-bang in the centre of Byron's viewfinder.

This was it. A rocket shot, captured on video. Just the thing to impress the people at *Kick-Off!* magazine! Rhoda drew back her foot, at the same time turning herself slightly to the side so that the camera would get the full effect of the blistering pace of her shot.

But, she remembered suddenly, her rocket shots usually saw her kicking the ball so hard she finished up losing her balance and sliding knees-down in the mud. She couldn't afford to do that, today!

Quickly she threw out her arms like a ballerina. She angled her wrists for extra grace. Looking straight at the camera Rhoda smiled her cheesiest smile – and let fly with her shot. But in looking at the camera, Rhoda had taken her eye off the ball. Instead of connecting with it cleanly on her instep, she caught it with the outside of her boot. Off fizzed the ball at a frightening pace – not at the goal, but straight at Daisy Higgins, who was still screaming in vain for a pass.

"Rhod-aaaaagggghh!"

Seeing the ball whizzing her way, Daisy dived to one side. She wasn't quick enough. The ball thumped against her leg, cannoned off…and flew straight into Byron, sending the valuable camcorder spinning from his hands!

Byron raced after it and picked it up. "You've broken it!" he yelled at Daisy, frantically punching different buttons on the camcorder.

"Don't blame me!" Daisy yelled back. "Blame Rhoda! I was just trying to get out of the way of her rotten shot!"

Byron twiddled another button, stuck his eye against the viewfinder, then breathed a sigh of relief. "No, it's still working. And the tape's all right. I haven't lost anything!"

"Hear that, Rhoda?" said Lennie, rubbing his hands together menacingly. "The tape's all right. You'll still be able to see yourself in action."

Rhoda didn't like to think about it. She knew what was on that tape.

"We all will," cackled Daisy. "We'll be able to have a good laugh at Rhoda's shocking shooting time after time after time!"

3

Safe and Sound

Rhoda walked glumly home. What a
disaster the session had been. For every good
shot of her, Byron had filmed something else
that was completely awful. She wouldn't be
asking Daisy's brother for a copy of *that* tape
to send to *Kick-Off!* magazine!

In fact, Rhoda really wished that tape could
be scrubbed altogether. Having her shocking
shooting exhibition shown on the youth
club's TV set every week didn't bear
thinking about!

By the time she'd reached the newsagents where she normally bought her magazine, Rhoda was feeling totally miserable. Perhaps treating herself to a fashion magazine would make her feel better. She was just about to tinkle open the door when, through the glass panel, she saw Lennie and Daisy about to come out. In no mood to be told about her performance again, Rhoda dived quickly round the corner to wait until they left.

But Lennie and Daisy didn't leave. They  stayed in the shop doorway, talking. And what Rhoda overheard made her hair stand on end! "Look!" said Lennie. "That's why Rhoda was playing to the camera all the time. She wants to be a model!"

How did he know? Rhoda peered round the corner. Because Lennie was a *Kick-Off!* reader too, that was how! He must have just bought his copy – and found her letter on the letters page!

"She'll find out about modelling if she tries the same thing against Leyton Lions on Saturday," snapped Daisy. "I'll model her backside with my boot!"

Lennie nodded thoughtfully. "The Lions are a good team. We'll need everybody concentrating on their game, not worrying if they look good. Maybe we should ask Byron to stay away."

"No, Lennie! I want Byron to finish that project fast. He's been getting on my nerves all week. He's scared of busting the camcorder and he still doesn't know what his advert's going to be about. Think of something else."

Rhoda sighed with relief. She wanted Byron there on Saturday, too. It would be her last chance to get some decent shots taken. But when she overheard the 'something else' that Lennie came up with, all thoughts of Saturday flew out of her head.

"I've got it!" said Lennie. "We get hold of Byron's tape...and tell Rhoda that if she doesn't pack in her posing we'll send a copy of it to *Kick-Off!* magazine..."

"Suggesting they publish some still pictures of Rhoda's shocking shooting," cried Daisy, excitedly. "Brilliant! If the thought of that doesn't stop her, nothing will..." Her voice drained away. "Oh, no."

"What's the problem?" asked Lennie.

"The problem is, Byron's terrified of breaking that camcorder. And having it knocked flying at training must have been the last straw."

"So? So?" squawked Lennie impatiently.

"So that's why he told me he wouldn't be walking home with me. I've just remembered. He said he was going to see Trev. To ask him to put the camcorder—"

Where? Where? Rhoda's ears were flapping so wildly she was having trouble keeping her feet on the ground.

"—in his big metal safe at the vicarage. The one that only Trev knows the combination to."

Rhoda had heard enough. Scurrying off in the opposite direction, she went back home and sat down for a good think.

At least if that tape was locked in Trev's safe it was out of harm's way. But only until Saturday, presumably. And not long after that Byron's project would be finished. He wouldn't need the tapes. He'd probably *give* them to Daisy! It could be shown at club night, sent to *Kick-Off!* magazine – or both!

Rhoda had to get her hands on that tape before then, and wipe it clean! But how?

She could think of only one way. Rhoda O'Neill, footballer and would-be model, was going to have to add a third talent to her collection. She was going to have to become a safe-cracker!

Trying to shield her hair from the pouring
rain, Rhoda raced up the path to the
vicarage and gave the bell push a firm
poke. No answer. She tried
again…and was on the
point of leaving when
Trev opened the door.

"Rhoda! I'm sorry
to keep you waiting.
This rain has got
me on bucket duty
trying to catch
the drips coming
through the holes
in the church roof."

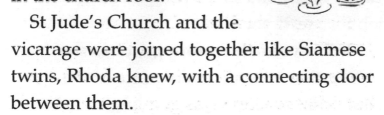

St Jude's Church and the
vicarage were joined together like Siamese
twins, Rhoda knew, with a connecting door
between them.

"That's all right, Trev," said Rhoda

brightly. "It's just that we've got a day off school today..."

It was true, too. Their teachers were off on one of their training days. The next bit wasn't quite so true. But it had been the only scheme Rhoda could think of to get her anywhere near Trev's study and the safe with Byron's camcorder in it.

"...So when I got up this morning, I thought to myself, I wonder if Trev needs any jobs done?" She smiled hopefully. "Do you? I could er...tidy your study, maybe? I'm really good at tidying. Expert, in fact!"

"Funnily enough," said Trev. "Mrs Dow, one of my regular cleaning ladies, has just called to say she's poorly. You could do her job for me, if you like."

"Tidies your study for you, does she?"

"No. She polishes every piece of the church silver until it positively gleams! You can do that if you like..."

Polishing? Rhoda hated polishing! She was ready to forget the whole thing and run for it when Trev added, "...I'll just get it all out of the safe."

Out of the safe? *The* safe! Open Sesame!

"Polishing?" squealed Rhoda. "Oh, I just *love* polishing. Lead me to it, Trev!"

The safe was a huge square thing. It had a dial on the front, and a large curved handle. Bending down, Trev twiddled the dial to the left, to the right, and to the left again. Then he tugged at the handle and the heavy door groaned open.

It was there! On the bottom shelf. Along with the glittering plates and shining cups

that Trev had started to pull out, sat Byron's camcorder! Trev had cracked the safe for her! And the best was yet to come.

"Here's the silver polish, Rhoda," said Trev. He handed over a bottle and a rag, then began  putting his coat on. "Now I'm afraid I'll have to leave you to look after things on your own. Any problems, call me at once. I'll be in the church."

"I understand, Trev," said Rhoda, trying to look serious.

The minute Trev left, she dived for the camcorder. Through the little window in the side she could see the tape. Strange. Byron seemed to have rewound it to the beginning. Why would he do that? Whatever the reason, it was very helpful.

All she had to do to record over Byron's shots of that awful practice game was to set the camcorder going, and put it back into the inky-black darkness of Trev's safe!

Rhoda's finger hovered over the record button. Should she do it? Wasn't erasing Byron's tape an unangelic thing to do? Yes, it was. But then Daisy and Lennie's plan to send it to *Kick-Off!* magazine must count as *two* unangelic acts – one each. So, by stopping them, she'd surely be doing two *angelic* acts, making the final score 2–1 in her favour!

Conscience settled, Rhoda quickly pressed the record button. She turned the camcorder round to look at the front. The little red light was glowing. It was recording!

Putting it carefully back into the safe, Rhoda shut the door. Now for an hour of silver polishing while that tape is being wiped clean, she thought. After all, one good clean deserved another!

And she would have attacked the job with a smile, but for one thing. At that moment she heard voices outside the door. Two voices. The voices of Lennie Gould and Daisy Higgins.

4

Caught in the Act!

Rhoda dived behind the curtains and peeped through the gap. Lennie and Daisy were looking around the room, mystified.

"Well, the silver's here," said Daisy, shaking the raindrops from her hair, "but where's Rhoda?"

How did they know I was here? wondered Rhoda. They must have seen Trev in the church. Maybe they'd also asked if he needed a job doing and Trev had told them about the safe and the silver as well. What a sneaky pair!

"She's not here, thank goodness," said Lennie.

"But the silver is," said Daisy, "so the safe's probably still unlocked. You keep watch while I look for that camcorder!"

Rhoda watched in horror as Daisy bent down, gripped the handle and tugged open the safe door. "There it is!" she cried.

Lennie knelt down beside her. "Why's that red light on?"

"Because it's recording," said Daisy. She frowned, then, in a sudden burst of wild panic, yelped, "Recording? Then it's recording us!"

"Recording us what?" cried Lennie.

"Recording you both opening Trev's safe," laughed Rhoda, stepping out from her hiding-place. "Naughty Lennie and naughty Daisy, caught in the act."

The two Angels players whirled round on her in stunned surprise. Seizing her chance Rhoda slammed the safe door shut, giving the dial on the front a good twiddle to make sure it was well and truly locked. "And that's the evidence safely shut away," she said.

Daisy glared at her. "You turned that camcorder on, didn't you?"

"I did," said Rhoda. "To rub out that training session before you sent it to *Kick-Off!* magazine. But now I don't have to worry, because in an hour's time the only faces on that tape will be yours. The moment Byron sees them, he'll be blaming you two for wiping his tape!"

She beamed triumphantly at Daisy and Lennie, expecting them to be looking as miserable as if they'd just lost 10–0 in a Cup Final. But they weren't.

"You admit you turned it on, then?" said Lennie.

"I certainly did," said Rhoda, pleased with herself. "I even checked the little red light to make sure."

Daisy guffawed. "Then your face will be on that tape as well as ours, Rhoda! Understand?"

Rhoda looked at the solidly locked safe door. "I get the picture," she groaned.

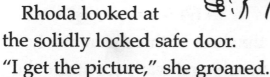

While they cleaned the church silver they discussed the problem. And, by the time they'd finished polishing, they'd polished off the problem as well!

"So we're agreed," said Rhoda. "As soon as Trev gives the camcorder back to Byron at the game tomorrow, we stick with him."

"The college loaned him two tapes," said Daisy. "Sooner or later he's bound to run out of tape, and swop the one with our faces on for a fresh one."

"And as soon as he takes it out, we'll grab it," said Lennie.

"And destroy it," said Rhoda firmly. "Agreed?"

"Agreed!"

The next day the three of them were ready for the Lions match, and waiting outside the changing rooms so that they could leap in the moment Trev handed Byron back the camcorder.

"All right, Byron?" said Rhoda anxiously.

Byron nodded. "Just got to change the battery for a freshly-charged one." He did so.

"Oh, yes. And check the tape's at the start..." At the start? Rhoda was confused. Surely Byron knew the tape was positioned at the start – he'd rewound it himself

before putting the camcorder in the safe.
Suddenly, Rhoda panicked. Oh, no!
Her tape-wiping trick would have left it
positioned at the end, wouldn't it?

"Yep," said Byron. "The tape's at the start."

It was? Phew! The camcorder must have
rewound automatically! Rhoda looked at
Byron expectantly. Was he going to take
the tape out and swop it for another one?
No, he wasn't. Instead, to Rhoda's
amazement, Byron lifted the camera and
started filming the other players running
out of the changing rooms!

Rhoda turned to Daisy and Lennie. "He's recording! From the start of that tape! But that means…"

Daisy grinned and nodded. "We won't need to pinch it – because the twit's wiping our faces out himself!"

"Yeah!" said Lennie happily. "We're in the clear!"

Wonderful! thought Rhoda. It no longer mattered that she'd ruined Byron's filming by rubbing out the shocking shooting tape. Dozy Byron would have done it himself anyway! She could get her portfolio shots today with a clear conscience!

So it was with renewed determination that Rhoda trotted carefully across to the pitch, avoiding the puddles and muddy patches caused by the torrential rain of the previous day.

Behind her, and equally determined, came Lennie and Daisy. "Right," said Daisy, "Byron kindly wiped us all off that tape. So if Rhoda the poser gets up to her tricks we can sort her out. Right?"

"Right," said Lennie. "How?"

Daisy sighed. "That's the problem. I don't know."

5

CUT!

Angels and Leyton Lions were two evenly-matched teams. Right from the kick-off, play swung from end to end. How it was still 0–0 at half-time, nobody knew. There'd been goalmouth scrambles, last-ditch tackles and, as the pitch became increasingly churned up, plenty of mistakes as players slipped in the mud.

At the referee's whistle, twenty-two players trooped off the pitch, twenty-one of them looking like accidents in a brown paint factory.

The odd one out was Rhoda. It had been agony, but she'd hardly touched the ball. She'd wanted to scramble and slide with the rest of them, but she'd simply had to stay clean for the sake of her portfolio. So whenever the ball had gone anywhere near Byron she'd run carefully towards it, smiled gaily for the benefit of the camcorder, then tiptoed out of the way again and left it for somebody like Lennie to come thundering in with a tackle.

"Think of something!" hissed Lennie to Daisy as they sucked their oranges. "It's like only having ten players!"

⚽   ⚽   ⚽

The second half began. Breaking forward, the Leyton wing-back came surging straight at Rhoda. Rather than risk getting dirty by tackling him, Rhoda began to back-pedal...until, with the Leyton player getting dangerously close to the Angels penalty area, Daisy was forced to slide in like a bulldozer and give away a free kick.

"Form a wall!"screeched Kirsten Browne, the Angels goalkeeper. Bazza Watts, Jeremy Emery, Tarlock Bhasin and Daisy all lined up and linked arms. Rhoda was just sneaking off when Kirsten screeched even louder, "A wall of five!"

54

Suddenly Rhoda felt herself yanked backwards by the collar. "Rhoda," growled Daisy, "you're needed! Stand next to me. And don't move!"

With Daisy looking in no mood to argue, Rhoda took her place at the end of the wall. In ran the Leyton striker to take the kick. He was going to blast it, Rhoda could tell. He was going to hammer that filthy, splodgy ball straight at the wall. In fact, straight at her!

Send a video to *Kick-Off!* magazine with a muddy-ball mark in the middle of her shirt? She couldn't. Quickly, Rhoda turned her back. That was no good, she realised at once. Having a round, brown splodge on her bottom would be even worse!

There was only one thing to do. As the Leyton striker thumped the kick, she skipped daintily to one side – allowing the ball to whizz through the gap she'd left and straight into the Angels goal. 1–0 to Leyton Lions!

"It's hopeless!" moaned Lennie. "She's scared of getting dirty."

"Getting dirty?" Daisy snapped her fingers in delight. "Why didn't I think of it before? If Rhoda gets dirty she won't want to be filmed, will she?"

Lennie didn't follow. "But she *isn't* getting dirty, is she?"

Daisy smiled menacingly. "Then we'll just have to make sure she does, won't we?"

The game went on. Tarlock won the ball with a good tackle and surged forward. "Attack!" yelled Lennie, as Tarlock played the ball on to Mick Ryall and the Angels winger set off on a mazy run.

Rhoda would have loved to surge towards the Leyton goal in the hope of getting in a flying header but, with a huge effort, she controlled herself. Instead of surging, Rhoda trotted elegantly into the

Leyton penalty area. Some pictures in the goalmouth would look great in her portfolio.

In came Mick's cross, skidding across the ground. Colly Flower slithered in with a Leyton defender, but both failed to get a touch. Jonjo Rix leapt for it and he missed it, too. Put off by all these mistakes the Leyton goalkeeper took his eye off the ball, letting it

squirt through his legs to stop right on his goal-line – no more than a touch away from Rhoda!

It was the easiest goal she'd ever scored in her life. All she had to do was stretch out a graceful boot, smile into the camcorder, and nudge the ball over the line to make the score 1–1...and give Daisy Higgins the idea she'd been searching for!

BOP!

Roaring upfield, the Angels defender flung her filthy hands round Rhoda's neck. "Goal!!!" she whooped, "Wa-hoo!!!"

Lennie Gould followed her lead. "Fantabuloso!!" he screamed, leaping on Rhoda's back and rubbing his filthy boots on her socks.

"Get off!" bawled Rhoda. "You're making me dirty!"

Worse was to come. Encouraged by Lennie and Daisy, the other Angels piled in too, leaping on to the growing pyramid until it collapsed into the muddy goal – with Rhoda

on the bottom! By the time she'd finally struggled free, she looked like a chocolate sponge that had melted!

She began to groan...only to discover that she didn't feel like groaning at all. She felt like jumping for joy. She didn't have to look her best any more. In fact, if that's what top models had to do all the time then they could keep it. Rhoda wanted to play her normal, all-action, mud-splattered game!

The game restarted. With a new heart, Rhoda sloshed into sliding tackles and flung herself into filthy interceptions. Leyton Lions didn't know what hit them. With just a couple of minutes to go, the Rhoda-inspired Angels were completely in control.

They won yet another corner. Positioning herself on the edge of the penalty area, Rhoda waited for Mick Ryall to swing the ball across. In she raced. Not fast enough, though! As the ball dropped towards a huge sea of mud, Rhoda realised that her only chance of reaching it was with a diving header.

Launching herself forward, she connected with the ball perfectly – then hit the ground to plough through the mud like an ocean liner!

Wiping the mud from her eyes, Rhoda looked up – and immediately noticed two things.

First, that her header had bulleted into the Leyton net!

And, second, that an excited Byron had his camcorder pointed straight at her!

"Fantastic!" he yelled as the referee's whistle blew to give Angels a 2–1 win, "I know what my advert's going to be about now! And guess what, Rhoda? You're going to be the star!"

The Angels were all gathered round the TV set in the club room. Linked to it through a spaghetti loop of cables was the camcorder. Trev turned out the lights, the TV flickered – and the world premier of Byron Higgins's advert began…

When it ended, Byron received the tumultuous applause with a bow. "Thank you," he said. "And thanks to Rhoda especially. She's going to be the star of part two as well."

"Part two?" said Rhoda, mystified.

Byron tapped the side of his nose. "Yes," he gurgled excitedly as he clicked another tape into the camcorder. "Part *two-oo!* My film of your training session."

Suddenly it sank in. The clean and tidy shot in the advert – that came from the first tape Byron had shot! It hadn't been wiped out!

Rhoda groaned. *That's* why the tape had been positioned at the start when she'd taken

66

the camcorder from Trev's safe – Byron must have replaced the training session tape with his spare one *before* he'd had the camcorder locked away!

Daisy had worked it out, too. She giggled in Rhoda's ear. "You wiped a tape that was blank to start with!"

"What you got to say about that, Rhoda?" hissed Lennie in the other ear.

Rhoda laughed. There was only one thing she could say. Cupping her hands round her mouth she called out, "Here it comes, folks! The shocking shooting show!"

FEARSOME FREE KICKS

CONTENTS

1

I'm Frozen

Jeremy Emery beat his arms across his
sparrow-like chest. He stamped
his feet on the ground. He
blew into his cupped
hands, then tucked them
tightly under his armpits.
"I am *frozen*!" he moaned.
Pulling his hands out
again, Jeremy rubbed
them together vigorously
until he thought he could feel

some warmth. Then he quickly transferred them to his face and carried on complaining from behind them.

"It's perishing! I've never been so cold in all my life. Why do we have to play football in the middle of winter? Eh? Tell me that! I feel like a polar bear with a crew cut!"

"Leave it out, Jez," said Lennie Gould, the Angels captain, "you can't be that cold!"

"Why can't I?" snapped Jeremy.

"Because we're still in the changing room!" yelled Lennie.

"Which means I'll be even colder outside!" Jeremy shouted back.

He pulled his fleece-lined jacket tight and burrowed his nose down into its collar. "If you lot want to play at being icebergs you can. I'm not training today."

"You are, Jez," said Lennie quietly.

"I'm not," said Jeremy, snuggling into the fleece lining like a gerbil. "Give me one good reason why I should."

"I'll do better than that. I'll give you twelve good reasons why you should. And here they are."

Jeremy peered out from his cocoon. Ranged behind Lennie were the other members of the Angels squad, all holding dripping cups.

"Everybody got their freezing cold water?" said Lennie. There were nods all round. "Good. Operation *Teach-Jeremy-What-It's-Really-Like-To-Be-An-Iceberg* ready for blast-off, then. On the count of three, let him have it. One, two, three..."

"All right, all right!" screeched Jeremy, leaping to his feet. "I'm getting changed!"

⚽   ⚽   ⚽

"Gather round, everybody!" yelled Trev. Trevor Rowe, the Angels coach, was standing on the edge of the penalty area, a football under his arm.

Jeremy groaned. All he wanted was for the session to end. Even after warm-up exercises, two laps of the training pitch and a practice game, he was still freezing.

Pulling his socks up over his knees and stuffing his hands down the legs of his shorts, the Angels defender moodily followed the others across to Trev.

"Right, then. I know it's half-term this week, but don't forget we've still got a big game on Saturday."

A game? thought Jeremy, in anguish. A *whole* game? In temperatures that would test a penguin? He'd never manage it.

"Er…are you sure the game will be on, Trev? I mean, they get called off at this time of year, don't they? Weather conditions and all that."

Trev smiled. "I doubt very much if this game will be called off, Jeremy. It's an invitation challenge match to celebrate the opening of the new Miller Park Sports Complex. We're very honoured to have been asked to be one of the sides."

"So who are we playing, Trev?" asked Rhoda O'Neill.

"Alton Swifts."

"Alton Swifts!" cried Jeremy. "But they're—"

"Tough tacklers," nodded Trev.

"Tough? They're the dirtiest team in dirty-land. The last time we played them we all spent more time on the ground than we did on our feet!"

"True. But as I always say—"

The whole squad knew what was coming next. As well as being their coach, Trev was vicar of St Jude's Church, and his saying about fair play was trotted out regularly. This time they beat him to it.

"Angels on and off the pitch!" chorused the whole squad.

"Don't worry, Trev," said Bazza Watts. "We'll beat them fair and square."

Jonjo Rix, one of the Angels front players, nodded. "Assuming we can get near their goal. They prefer to foul us and give away free kicks outside their penalty area."

"Which is why we're going to practise them now!" said Trev. "To make them count on Saturday!" He tossed the ball to Jonjo. "Jonjo, you can go first. The rest of you form a wall."

As he joined the wall, Jeremy felt totally miserable. He didn't want to play on Saturday. He didn't want to get his ankles kicked and land in a heap on a frosty, bone-hard pitch. He didn't want to practise free kicks now, either. He didn't want to be anywhere near a football pitch because he was *frozen*!

With a sudden, irritable action, Jeremy swung his arms wide, ready to warm himself by flapping them against his chest.

"Ow!" cried Tarlock Bhasin as Jeremy's left hand caught him on the nose.

"Oy!" shouted Lulu Squibb as Jeremy's right hand hit her behind the ear.

Trev frowned. "Maybe you'd be better at the end of the wall, Jeremy."

Jeremy moved – slowly. His feet were like blocks of ice. He tried stamping them as he moved.

"Ow! Ow! Ow!" shouted Colly Flower, Daisy Higgins and Ricky King as he stamped on their toes in quick succession.

"Jeremy," sighed Trev. "Why don't you try the first free kick, before you crock the whole team?"

Crock the whole team? Trev's joke gave Jeremy an idea. If he was crocked himself, he wouldn't have to play! It wouldn't be difficult. He could pretend to slip and twist his ankle as he took the free kick. Perfect!

Changing places with Jonjo, Jeremy got ready to take the kick. Ahead of him was the Angels wall with a crouching Kirsten Browne in the goal behind them.

"Let's see something special, Jeremy," said Trev, then blew his whistle.

Jeremy had it all worked out. In he ran. Reaching the ball, he deliberately let his left foot turn to the side. Even as he kicked the ball he was sinking to the ground, ready to let loose his planned wail of agony.

And then he saw the ball. Curling perfectly over the wall, his free kick was dipping and swinging far beyond the reach of Kirsten and into the top corner of the net!

"Aaggh…goal!!!"

"Looks like we've found our free-kick specialist," said Trev when they finally got back to the changing room.

"Yeah, fearsome free kick, Jez!" called Lennie Gould.

Jeremy sighed and shivered at the same time. A fearsome free kick hadn't been what he'd intended to take. Neither had he meant to leap to his feet and jump for joy, thus ruining his own plan for getting out of Saturday's match.

"You're sure this game will be on, then?" he said glumly. "The referee could call it off."

Trev shook his head. "Not a chance, Jeremy. But thank you for reminding me about the referee. I must get a special referee's trophy made up to mark the occasion. Now, what was the ref's name again?"

The coach flipped open the notebook in which he kept every scrap of information about the team and their matches.

"Nicholas," said Trev, finding the page he'd been

looking for. "A new referee, recently moved to the area. In fact…to your road, Jeremy. Number 9, Rosemary Avenue."

"Really?" said Jeremy. "Fancy that."

Or *not* fancy that, perhaps? wondered Jeremy. Maybe this Mr Nicholas was the sort who didn't fancy running around in the freezing cold either. Maybe he could be persuaded that it would be a rotten idea to allow this match against Alton Swifts to go ahead and much more enjoyable to stay at home in front of a roaring fire.

Pulling his fleece-lined jacket tightly about him, the Angels defender headed hopefully out into the icy wind.

He hadn't quite worked out how, but before too long Mr Nicholas and he were going to have a little chat – about the weather!

2

I'm Frozen Too!

Jeremy sat thoughtfully next to the bubbling
radiator in the lounge, a fleece-lined
dressing-gown around his shoulders and a
huge pair of fleece-lined slippers on his feet.

What he needed was an excuse to visit Mr
Nicholas – ideally, an excuse that would let him
draw the referee's attention to how cold it was.

"You may not like the cold weather, love,"
said Mrs Emery from behind her sewing
machine in the corner of the room, "but it's
very good for business!"

Jeremy's mum worked from home, making fleece-lined clothing. Hats, coats, cardigans, jackets – you name it, Mrs Emery could make it with a soft, warm, cosy fleece lining. People would write or ring her with their orders and she would make what they wanted.

She'd had a busy day. On one side of her a tottering pile of finished orders was wrapped and waiting to be posted. On her other side sat a bulging bag of fleecy scraps ready for the dustbin.

Still stuck for an idea, Jeremy wandered over to watch his mum work. He'd seen her put so many linings in things over the years he reckoned he could probably do it himself, now.

"Do you want me to wrap that for you?" he asked as Mrs Emery finished off an amazingly chunky and warm-looking cardigan.

"Not this one," said his Mum. "This one's not for posting. It's for a house in our road."

Jeremy's heart leapt. "Not...number 9, by any chance?"

Mrs Emery checked her order sheet. "Yes, as it happens. Name of Nicholas. I'll take it down later..."

The garment was almost snatched from her hand. Pausing only to shout, "I'll take it for you!" Jeremy hurried out of the door and down the road.

As he cradled Mrs Emery's finest work, hope burned inside him. A referee ordering chunky fleece-lined cardigans had to be a referee who felt the cold!

⚽　　　⚽　　　⚽

The door was answered almost before the bell stopped chiming. Opening by the merest fraction, a bearded, well-built man peered out through the tiny gap.

"Mr Nicholas?" asked Jeremy.

"Yes. What is it? You're letting the cold in."

"I'm Mrs Emery's son. I've brought your—"

Jeremy wasn't given a chance to finish. In a flash the door was opened, he was yanked inside, and the door was shut again.

"Quick!" hissed the man. "While my wife is upstairs in the bath!"

Jeremy glanced up the stairs. He just had time to notice the clothes-horse on the landing, with a referee's kit laid out on it to dry, before the man pushed him down the hallway and into a small study with a heater going full blast. Even so, he slipped on the fleecy cardigan and gave a sigh of pleasure.

"Sorry about the panic," he said to Jeremy. "It's just that I don't want Maisie – Mrs Nicholas – to know I'm getting this."

"Why not?"

"Because she'll think I'm a weed. She doesn't understand what it's like to be cold. She's one of these fresh-air fiends. Loves the stuff. Me – I hate it!"

Jeremy's mouth fell open in surprise. It could have been himself talking! "Really? You don't like the cold then?"

"No I do not!" Mr Nicholas shuddered, then patted the cardigan. "That's why I ordered this. To wear it at weekends. It'll be perfect for the football matches."

A referee in a cardigan? For a moment Jeremy's mind boggled – then came quickly back to the reason for his visit as the man added gloomily, "It's Miller Park this weekend."

"Yes, I know. Angels FC against Alton Swifts." Jeremy took a deep breath. "You don't think it'll be too cold, do you? Cold enough to call it off?"

"I hope so," said Mr Nicholas.

"You do?"

"I certainly do. Even with this lovely cardigan on it'll be no fun." For some reason he lowered his voice. "You haven't seen the weather forecast, I suppose? Some snow would help."

"Snow?" Jeremy's eyes lit up. "You mean the game would be off if there was some snow before Saturday?"

"Snow has done the trick before," said Mr Nicholas. "Or a hard frost leaving lashings of ice. Anything to show it would be really slippery underfoot. That's what would make all the difference."

He sounded almost dreamy, until the sound of an upstairs door being opened stirred him into action. Quickly he ushered Jeremy out of the house.

"Keep your fingers crossed," he hissed as the Angels player hurried away.

I'm going to do more than keep my fingers crossed, thought Jeremy, unable to believe the conversation had gone so well. A referee who couldn't stand cold weather either!

Already a plan was forming. If Referee Nicholas needed some snow and ice before he could call the game off, then snow and ice was what he was going to get! Bucketfuls of it!

3

Jeremy Plays it Cool

Friday evening, decided Jeremy. That's when to do it. If he could convince Mr Nicholas that the weather had taken a turn for the worse on Friday evening, the referee would surely decide that there was little chance of it improving in time for the match. He would probably call the game off by telephone there and then!

That also gave Jeremy the best part of two days to prepare – time that he would definitely need for what he had in mind.

First thing Thursday morning, Jeremy bundled himself up in as many layers of clothing as he could and went out into the garage. After a morning spent there he visited the dustbin, then came back inside, took off the layers, and spent the first part of the afternoon in his room. Then it was back on with the layers and out into the garage again.

The pattern was repeated on Friday. Garage, room, garage – until, as dusk approached, he was ready. The minute Mrs Emery departed for her usual Friday evening outing to the cinema, Jeremy raced up to his room. Moments later he came down carrying the bulging bag of white flakes he'd spent hours making by chopping up some of the fleecy lining scraps he'd retrieved from the dustbin.

Snow is definitely on the way! thought
Jeremy cheerfully.

And ice! Out he went to the garage – to
the freezer that lived there, and in which
he'd spent even more hours preparing a
small mountain of ice cubes. Loading them
all into a wheelbarrow, Jeremy began
to trundle it down the road towards
number nine.

Suddenly, he stopped. A tall figure,
dressed in a track suit and with long hair
flowing behind her, had just bounded down
the path and stopped at the gate.

Mrs Nicholas! realised Jeremy. Going
for a jog! Her husband was right. She *was*
a fresh-air fiend!

But – it was helpful. With her out of the way for a while he could put his plan into practice in the certain knowledge that it would have to be the referee who'd answer the door.

As Mrs Nicholas jogged away round the corner, Jeremy trundled the barrow up to the front door of number nine – and tipped out his load of ice cubes. Clutching his bag of fleecy flakes, he then shinned up a broad-branched tree nearby.

"Snow, or lashings of ice," Mr Nicholas had said. Jeremy looked down at the path, now looking like a skating rink. Well, he'd certainly given the referee plenty of ice. Now for the snow!

He inched along a branch until he could see into the study he'd been in the other day. Perfect! Mr Nicholas was there, his back to the window.

His back to the window? That was no good. How would he see the snow fall that way? He had to get Mr Nicholas to turn round. But how? By adding a howling gale, of course!

"Wooooooooooo!" went Jeremy loudly and, he hoped, sounding like a gale.

In the study, Mr Nicholas looked up. Encouraged, Jeremy let loose a handful of flakes, then, as they drifted realistically past the study window, let rip with some gale-force blasts.

"Woooooo! Wooooooooo! Woooooooooo! Wooooooooooooooooooooooooooooooo!!"

Had he not been making so much noise, he might have heard Mrs Nicholas return panting from her short jog. As it was, the first he knew of it was when his own howls were drowned by an even louder commotion.

"Eeeeekkk!" howled Mrs Nicholas as she

jogged through her front gate and suddenly slipped on a layer of ice that hadn't been there when she left.

"Oooohhh!" howled Mrs Nicholas as she slithered up the path and rammed into Jeremy's tree, causing him to lose his grip on the bag of fleecy flakes.

"Aaaahhh!" Mrs Nicholas howled as Jeremy's flakes cascaded down on top of her...until, for some reason, this particular howl turned into a succession of sneezes. "Aaaaahhh...choo! Aaaaahhh-choo! Aaaaahhh-choo!"

Why this should be, Jeremy couldn't imagine. What he soon saw, however, was that where his gale impersonations had failed, Mrs Nicholas's sneezing had succeeded. Hearing the commotion outside, Mr Nicholas rushed to the door – and promptly slipped over to join his wife in the middle of the path.

It was, Jeremy decided, time to make his point and leave. Dropping from the branches, he slithered over to the referee and began to help him to his feet.

"Slippery underfoot, isn't it, Mr Nicholas? Too dangerous for football, I'd say. What with this snow and all I don't reckon you've got much choice. Angels FC versus Alton Swifts – match postponed. A responsible referee like you can't make any other decision!"

The bearded man gave him a blank look. "A responsible *what* like me?"

"Referee!"

Mr Nicholas shook his head. "I'm not a referee. What on earth gave you that idea?"

"But...our ref's named Nicholas and you said you go to football matches at weekends...Miller Park this week..."

"Yes, I know. But I don't go to referee. I go to *watch* the referee."

"Meaning me," growled Mrs Nicholas in Jeremy's ear. "*I'm* your referee on Saturday. A-tishoo!"

Jeremy swung round, his mouth open. A lady referee! More than that, a fresh-air fiend of a lady referee who thought nothing of going out jogging whatever the weather!

"Then...ha-ha..." Jeremy laughed weakly, "I don't suppose you think it's a bit on the nippy side for football?"

"No, I do not! A-tishoo!"

"The game will be on then? The pitch at Miller Park won't be too slippery?"

"The pitch at Miller Park?" Mrs Nicholas gave Jeremy a curious look. "Of course not—"

She was about to say something else when another mighty sneeze erupted. Suspiciously, she picked up a couple of the 'snowflakes' and held them under her nose.

"Fleece!" she roared. "That's why I'm sneezing. Fleece always makes me – aaaaaa-tishoooooooo!!"

It was definitely time to move. As quickly as he could, Jeremy began to scuttle his way along the path – only to tread on a solid clump of ice cubes and fly into the air himself!

The next thing he knew, Mrs Nicholas was bending over him, her curious look now replaced by one that was very, very nasty.

"Oh, yes," she growled. "Your game will be on. Because the Miller Park pitch won't be covered in ice cubes. Nor will there be flurries of snow made out of this stuff. A-tishoo!"

Jeremy didn't bother to struggle to his feet. Still on his hands and knees he half crawled and half slid to the front gate.

"See you tomorrow," shouted Mrs-referee-Nicholas after him. "And take my advice. Wrap up really, really warm! A-tishoo!"

4

A Frosty Reception

Wrap up really, really warm? Even as he dashed indoors, Jeremy wondered why he hadn't thought of it before.

Racing up to his room he grabbed the fleecy scraps left over from his snow-making exercise. He would use them to sew a fleecy lining into his Angels football kit!

Jeremy dived back downstairs to his mum's sewing machine. After watching her in action so often, he knew exactly what to do. Turning his football kit inside out, he began work.

First, he sewed a thick, fleecy lining to his shorts.

Then he lined both his socks. No chilly toes tomorrow, thought Jeremy!

He then gave his shorts another layer of lining for good luck.

Finally, he started work on his shirt. Picking an extra thick slice of fleece, he stitched it into place. Would that be enough? If he'd given his shorts a double dose, perhaps he should do the same for his shirt as well.

With a satisfied nod, he stitched on a second layer. It was a bit of a struggle – but finally he managed it.

Then, together with his trainers to cope with what was bound to be a bone-hard pitch, Jeremy squeezed it all into his sports bag.

Tucking himself into his comfortable, warm bed, Jeremy settled down happily. The game held no fears for him now. Miller Park? They could be playing Alton Swifts at North Pole Park for all he cared.

He, Jeremy 'Hot Stuff' Emery, had got his own central heating system!

⚽   ⚽   ⚽

And when he emerged from the Miller Park dressing rooms the following afternoon, it certainly looked like it. With his layers of lining, Jeremy looked more like a heavyweight boxer than a footballer.

He'd got there early, wanting to make sure that his altered kit was going to do the trick. If not, he wanted to have enough time to arrange the extra scraps of fleece he'd brought along just in case.

Jeremy stepped outside. It was as cold a day as there'd been all week, and there was a stiff breeze blowing as well. But he felt like a piece of toast! His design was a roaring success!

"I see you took my advice," said a voice from behind him. "And got yourself dressed up nice and warm."

It was Mrs Nicholas, in her black referee's kit. Her *thin* black referee's kit. Jeremy couldn't believe it.

"So why didn't you?" he asked. "You're going to be freezing in that gear."

Mrs Nicholas smiled, nastily. "No, I'm not."

Forget fresh-air fiend, thought Jeremy,

she's a fresh-air lunatic! "Well, I think I prefer my kit to yours," he laughed. "It's freezing out here."

"You're right, it is," said Mrs Nicholas. "But the match isn't being played out here."

"What?"

The referee's nasty smile grew even nastier. "Why do you think I was so sure the match would go ahead? This is an invitation game, remember. To celebrate the completion of the new Miller Park Sports Complex – part of which includes a junior-sized indoor football pitch."

Jeremy gulped. *"Indoor* football pitch?"

"That's right," cackled Mrs Nicholas. "And dressed like that I can tell you're going to have an absolutely scorching game!"

5

Hot Stuff!

Jeremy soon discovered how right she was.

With his extra padding, he'd started to feel warmer than warm during their pre-match kick-in on the new indoor pitch. The other Angels had noticed it, of course.

"Hey, Jez," called Bazza Watts. "You all right? You look a bit puffed out."

"And puffed up," said Tarlock Bhasin. "Have you put on weight, Jez?"

"A bit," lied Jeremy, unable to admit how stupid he'd been. "Been eating more to build up my strength for the winter months. Y'know, like polar bears do."

Bazza frowned. "Yeah? Well from here it looks like you've been overeating!"

Jeremy may not have been overeating, but very soon he was overheating. Once Mrs Nicholas had blown her whistle to set the game in motion, things rapidly got worse.

After five minutes, he felt like he was wearing an overcoat in the middle of a steamy jungle. His face was glistening with perspiration.

After ten minutes he felt like he'd been staked out in the middle of the Sahara Desert – again wearing an overcoat. Perspiration was dripping off his nose.

And after fifteen minutes...after fifteen minutes it didn't feel like he was wearing an overcoat at all. It felt like he was inside a volcano that was about to erupt.

No, it was worse. It felt like he *was* a
volcano, but one that was bubbling over
with perspiration instead of lava.

"Getting a little hot under the collar are
we?" Mrs-referee-Nicholas whispered in his
ear as Alton Swifts won a corner. "Perhaps
you should have held on to some of your
ice cubes instead of spreading them all over
my path!"

"I apologise!" panted the boiling Jeremy.

"It's too late for apologies. Because of you, my husband has got a bruised bottom – too bruised for him to get out of his study chair and do our shopping, so he says!"

"I'll do your shopping," moaned Jeremy. "Just let me take this shirt off! I'll play without one on."

Mrs Nicholas shook her head. "Sorry. That would be completely against the rules. You'll just have to suffer."

Out on the right, the Swifts were about to take the corner they'd won. Next to Jeremy, their striker started bobbing up and down as he waited for the ball to be swung over. Suddenly, he collapsed in a heap.

Peeeeeep!

Whistle in her mouth, Mrs Nicholas came running over – then pointed to the penalty spot!

"What for?" cried Jeremy. "I didn't touch him! He slipped over!"

The referee pointed down at the puddle of perspiration beside Jeremy's feet. "Yes – because of that! And who's responsible for it? You! Penalty to the Swifts!"

Seconds later the penalty had been hammered past Kirsten Browne in the Angels goal to put Swifts 1–0 ahead.

"How do you feel now, Jeremy?" laughed Mrs Nicholas on her way back to the centre circle. "A bit of a drip?"

Lennie Gould came hurrying over. "Have you done something to annoy her? She's giving us nothing."

It was true. Whenever the Angels had swept on to the attack, the Swifts defenders had regularly halted them with fouls. Not once, though, had they been awarded a free kick in anything like a dangerous position.

Lulu Squibb added a grumble of her own. "Even when we do get through, that goalkeeper of theirs stops us. He's playing a blinder."

That was true, too. The Swifts goalie had already tipped a great shot from Colly Flower over the bar and an even better one from Rhoda O'Neill round the post.

The pattern continued way into the second half. By mopping his face and legs at every opportunity, Jeremy had at least managed to avoid creating any more troublesome puddles of perspiration.

At the other end, though, the Angels had come no closer to finding the Swifts net. With their goalkeeper still playing brilliantly and Mrs Nicholas still refusing to award the Angels free kicks, time was running out.

"Go up and join the attack, Jez," called Lennie as Mick Ryall forced a corner on the right. "Maybe another body will make all the difference!"

Jeremy gasped his way forward. Another body would certainly make all the difference to him! The one he'd got was rapidly reaching boiling point. If he didn't do something soon, he'd melt.

Of course! Why hadn't he thought of it before? What had gone in could just as easily come out! Jeremy lifted his shirt and began tearing at the fleecy lining. By the time Mick Ryall was running in to take the corner, he'd already ripped out a handful.

Tossing it aside, Jeremy began to tear out more and more, scattering it everywhere, forgetting everything else, until suddenly…

Over came Mick's corner kick.

Up rose Colly Flower to meet it with a powerful header.

Off flashed the ball towards the Swifts net…

"A-tishoooooo!!" came a mighty sneeze from beside Jeremy as Mrs Nicholas found herself in the middle of a violent fleece storm.

Out from between her lips shot the referee's whistle…

And across dived the Swifts brilliant
goalkeeper to catch it as Colly's header flew
into the other corner of his net for the
Angels to equalise!

There was nothing Mrs Nicholas could
do about it. With a mumbled apology to
the Swifts goalkeeper she retrieved her
whistle and blew for the goal. But on the
way back to the centre circle she collared
Jeremy.

"Take that – a-tishoo! – shirt off –
a-tishoo!"

Jeremy grinned, then repeated exactly what she'd said to him earlier. "Sorry. As you said yourself, Mrs Nicholas, that would be completely against the rules. Like me, you'll just have to suffer!"

And suffer Mrs Nicholas did, sneezing her head off whenever Jeremy ripped out more fleece in an effort to cool himself down. Not that he wasn't suffering too.

As the game entered its last minute, Jeremy still felt like a furnace with a fever.

There was only one thing left to do. As he joined one final Angels attack, Jeremy started de-fleecing his shorts.

Ahead of him, Jonjo Rix had the ball. Across flew one of the rugged Alton Swifts defenders. Launching himself into a tackle, the defender sent Jonjo flying.

"Foul, Ref!" cried Lulu Squibb.

"Play on!" roared Mrs Nicholas, now even more determined not to give the Angels any free kicks. "A-tishoo!" she sneezed, before clamping the whistle between her teeth again.

Behind her, Jeremy was still struggling with the lining of his shorts. He'd sewn the fleece to the elastic round the waist and he couldn't shift it.

"Yeee-ess!"

With a final desperate effort, Jeremy ripped away both fleece and elastic – tossing it all aside just as the ball ran loose to Colly Flower on the edge of the Swifts penalty area and he, too, was hacked down.

"Foul, Ref!" cried Lulu Squibb again. "A-peeeeeeeeeeep-choo!"

As the fleecy lining of Jeremy's shorts had sailed by, Mrs Nicholas hadn't had time to remove the whistle from between her teeth before she'd sneezed again. She'd blown for a free kick without meaning to!

Lennie raced up to Jeremy's shoulder. "You take it, Jez. Fearsome free kick into the top corner. Just like you did in training!"

"But..." began Jeremy.

How could say he hadn't meant to score in training, he'd meant to slip over and pretend to be injured? He couldn't. But neither could he remember how he'd done it!

Placing the ball, Jeremy took a few steps back. There was only one thing to do. He was just going to have to try and score properly.

In he ran – only to feel his shorts, now without most of their elastic, begin to slip down!

Still running, Jeremy snatched at them
with his hand. He was too late. As he
reached the ball, his shorts were down to his
knees. Unable to stop himself, Jeremy
stumbled – perfectly!

His left foot turned to the side – just as it
had in training.

Tangled up in the shorts he sank to the
ground at the same moment as he kicked
the ball – just like he had in training.

And finally, just as it had in training,
the ball curled perfectly over the Alton
Swifts wall to dip and swing far beyond
their goalkeeper and into the top corner
of the net!

2–1 to Angels!

A-tishoo! Peeep! A-tishoo! Peeep!
A-tishoo! Peeep!

As a thoroughly miserable Mrs Nicholas
blew for the goal and, soon after, for
full-time, the boiling Jeremy didn't hesitate.
Racing from the pitch, he headed for the
nearest door.

The others found him outside, standing in the freezing wind, his arms wide and a broad smile on his face.

"Jez! What are you doing?" yelled Lennie Gould.

"What does it look like?" gasped the still steaming Jeremy. "I'm chilling out!"

WICKED
WINGERS

CONTENTS

1

Superior Skill

"Leave him to me, guys!"

Bazza Watts, the Angels right-back, jogged confidently out towards the wiry boy dribbling the ball his way. Angels FC were playing a team named Maddox Rebels and the boy with the ball was the Rebels' star winger Dylan Thompson, otherwise known as Twister Thompson because he usually had the defender marking him tied up in knots.

But not today. The Angels were 3–0 ahead and Bazza was having a great game.

What's more, he was making sure
that everyone knew it – especially
his opponent.

"Come on, Twister, let's see if you can
do better this time," he yelled at Thompson
as the winger dribbled nearer. "Twentieth
time lucky!"

Bringing the ball close, Twister ducked
low and feinted to go to Bazza's right. But
Bazza wasn't fooled. He'd seen every one of
Twister's tricks so often in the
school playground that he
knew exactly what was
coming next. And so,
waiting until the Rebels
winger made his move
and tried to dribble
past, Bazza hit him with
a crunching tackle that
sent both the ball and
player flying into touch.

"So that's why they call you 'Twister'," laughed Bazza. "'Cos you're so good at somersaults!"

Glaring angrily, Thompson picked himself up. "Gimme the ball!" he screeched to his team-mate taking the throw-in. "His luck can't last!"

Bazza laughed again. "Luck? It's not luck, Twister. It's skill. Superior skill."

Bringing the ball under control, Thompson dribbled forward again. Ahead of him, Bazza yawned. "Come on then. Bet you five pounds you can't get past me."

"Five pounds?"

"Five lovely pounds," repeated Bazza, grinning. "But try something different this time, eh? The bet's off if I get so bored I fall asleep."

"Right!" snarled Thompson. "You're on. Say goodbye to your money, Wattso!"

Gritting his teeth with determination, Twister stepped his left foot over the ball in an attempt to send Bazza the wrong way. The Angels full-back didn't move.

"Bo-ring," sighed Bazza.

Thompson tried again. He twisted to his right. Bazza went with him. He dummied to sprint forward. Bazza didn't move. He darted forward. Bazza was in position at once, blocking his way.

"Give in, yet?" laughed Bazza.

Desperately, Thompson tried the only trick he hadn't tried – putting his foot under the ball to scoop it up into the air and over Bazza's head.

The Angels defender saw it coming. The instant Twister's foot went under the ball, Bazza sailed in with a tackle like a sledge-hammer – and Thompson sailed into the air again, to turn another perfect somersault!

"You want to take up high-diving, Twister! You'd get full marks every time!"

Thompson scowled at the Angels full-back. "You're going to pay for this, Wattso."

"Wrong, Twister," laughed Bazza as the referee's whistle shrieked, "You're the one who's going to be doing the paying. That's full-time, and you didn't get past me – so I win the bet!"

"You don't mean it? I haven't got five pounds!"

"Sorry, Twister, a bet's a bet. Tell you what, I'll give you a couple of days to raise the money. You can give it to me Wednesday. A nice crisp five pound note will do nicely!"

⚽   ⚽   ⚽

"You had a good game Bazza," said Tarlock Bhasin in the changing rooms afterwards.

"Good?" snorted Bazza. "I wasn't good, Tarlock, I was brilliant! Twister didn't get past me once."

"Only because he couldn't get round your big head without taking the ball out of play," said Lulu Squibb.

"Out of the country, you mean," laughed Colly Flower.

"You're just jealous, Lulu," said Bazza. "Jealous of my superior skill."

Lulu's eyes flashed. "Superior skill? You big banana, I've got more skill in my pigtails than you've got in your whole body! I'll beat you at anything!"

"You want to bet?"

"Yeah!" shouted Lulu. "Name it!"

But before Bazza could do just that, the argument was interrupted by Trev, the Angels coach, calling them to attention.

"Training on Tuesday!" he called. "And I'll be trying something new."

"What's that, Trev?" asked Lennie Gould, the team captain, excitedly.

In real life their coach was the vicar of St Jude's Church, but it had always been said that he'd been a good enough footballer to turn professional if he hadn't wanted to be a vicar more. So when Trev talked football they all listened.

"Throw-ins," said Trev.

"Throw-ins?" echoed Mick Ryall, disappointed. "Great. Not."

"*Long* throw-ins," said Trev, emphasising the "long". "We're playing Welby Wolves next week and they're not so hot at defending crosses from the right. So I want to surprise them by aiming some long throw-ins at them as well – which means finding out who's got the longest throw."

The moment Trev left the room, Bazza turned back to Lulu. "So you can beat me at anything, can you?"

"Anything!" snapped Lulu, jutting out her chin defiantly. "You name it, Bragger Watts, and I can beat you at it!"

"In that case, I bet you…"

"Bet me?" gulped Lulu.

Bazza nodded, smiling. Offering to bet Twister Thompson out on the pitch had been a bit of an accident, the words slipping out in the heat of the moment. But having won that bet, Bazza found himself simply unable to resist trying to win another one – especially when the idea he'd just had was a sure-fire certainty.

"Yes, I bet you…five pounds! That my throw-in will be longer than your throw-in."

Lulu snorted. "So that's what you want to bet, is it?"

She moved threateningly close to Bazza, jabbing her finger at his chest.

"Well let me tell you, Bazza the Bighead…" Jab. "Nothing would give me greater pleasure than to take your money…" Jab. "So the answer is…"

"Yes?" said Bazza eagerly.

"Er…no," replied Lulu. She turned away.

"No?" sneered Bazza. "No? Why not?"

"Because a chimpanzee like you could beat me at throw-ins with one hand tied behind your back," snapped Lulu. "You know it – and so do I!"

2

I'll Knock your Block off!

Bazza walked home lost in thought. What a pity Lulu hadn't let her temper get the better of her and accepted his challenge. The prospect of another winning bet had really excited him – and still did.

He was certain he could produce a longer throw-in than Lulu. He was a big and muscular boy. She was a titchy, weedy girl with a fire-cracker for a brain. Of course he could beat her. Even she thought he could. What had she said? *"You could beat me at*

145

throw-ins with one hand tied behind your back."

A slow smile crossed Bazza's face. One hand tied behind his back? Yes, that was how to do it…

Lulu was already on her way out of the changing room when Bazza turned up for the practice session on Tuesday night. When she saw the Angels defender, she stopped dead.

"What have you done to yourself?" she gasped.

Bazza's wrist was bandaged and his arm nestled in a huge white sling. "I don't want to talk about it," he groaned.

"Good job I didn't bet you about the throw-in competition then, wasn't it?" said Lulu.

"Why?" replied Bazza, looking as though he didn't understand.

"Because with a bad wrist, you don't stand a chance of beating me. So if that bet was on, I'd be about to take your money."

Bazza snorted. "You? Take my money? You must be joking! I could have one arm in plaster and the other held on by sticky tape and I'd still be able to take a longer throw-in than you!"

"Oh you would, would you?" retorted Lulu, her pigtails swinging threateningly.

"Easy-squeezy, double-sneezy," said Bazza. "I'm still prepared to bet you."

"Oh you are, are you?" yelled Lulu, almost bursting with rage. "Right, a bet it is! Get ready to kiss your five pounds goodbye!"

Trev got the competition under way right at the start of the session. Lining the squad up along the right touchline, he drew lots for the order they'd take their throws. Lulu's name came out of the hat last, with Bazza's immediately before hers.

"You'll know you can't win before you even pick up the ball," hissed Bazza.

"I'll know I've got nothing to beat, you mean," snapped Lulu.

148

Each of the squad took three throw-ins, aiming the ball as far as they could into the goal mouth. In each case, Trev stuck a small marker into the ground to show where their best throw had landed.

As his turn drew near, Bazza had a good look at what he had to beat.
The nearest marker belonged to Lionel Murgatroyd. He'd been credited with a one-metre throw for trying, after the ball had slipped out of his hands and actually ended up behind him!

The markers for Jonjo Rix, Rhoda O'Neill, Tarlock Bhasin and Daisy Higgins were all pretty level, each of them having managed to get their throws as far as the edge of the penalty area.

A metre or so further away were the markers for Colly Flower, Mick Ryall and Jeremy Emery, with those for Kirsten Browne and Lennie Gould another metre beyond them.

Ahead of them all, though, was Ricky King's. After an opening foul, when he'd forgotten he couldn't use just one hand as he used to when he was playing American Football[1] and had launched the ball on to the roof of the changing room, he'd managed to get a legal throw-in almost as far as the edge of the six-yard box.

"Good one, Ricky," called Trev. "Your turn, Bazza. Do your best."

"Not that it'll be good enough," said Lulu.

"No?" smirked Bazza. "I bet it will be good enough. Especially when—"

Shrugging his arm out of its sling, Bazza whirled it cheerfully round and round like a high-speed windmill.

"Wha— wha—" gurgled Lulu as she realised she'd been tricked. "You cheating stinker! You said you'd hurt your arm!"

"No I didn't," said Bazza innocently. "You asked me what I'd done to myself, and I said I didn't want to talk about it. And I didn't!"

"But – but – the bet..."

"Is on!" cried Bazza. "Watch this for a throw-in, Lulu!"

Picking up the ball, Bazza took a few steps back from the touchline and ran in for his first throw. It was a corker. Sailing out of his hands it flew past Ricky's marker to land almost level with the near goalpost!

"I think that should be good enough," he smirked. "I won't bother about my other two throws. Your go, Lulu."

And with that he swaggered off across to where Trev was placing his marker. By the time he got there, Lulu was winding up for her first throw. With a huff and a puff she ran in and heaved the ball a good five metres short of Bazza's mark.

"Not a bad try," called Bazza, before adding, "a terrible one!"

Snatching up another ball, Lulu steamed up for her second throw. In spite of all her effort it got no further than the first one.

"Hopeless!" hooted Bazza. "Call that a throw-in? Lulu Squibb, you couldn't throw a party!"

Doubling up with laughter, he hardly noticed as the seething Lulu grabbed her third ball and stomped backwards for her longest run-up yet. He only realised that she was about to take her final throw when she roared up to the touchline like a steam train, stopped, whirled her arms over in a blur and, with a window-rattling cry of "Yaaaaaahhhhhh!!!" launched the ball straight at his head!

Bazza didn't have a moment to lose. As the ball zoomed towards him like a shot fired from a cannon, he dived out of the way.

"Missed me!" he laughed, scrambling to his feet. "Rotten shot!"

"More's the pity," yelled Lulu, running over.

"No it wasn't, Lulu," laughed Lennie, "If you'd hit him, your throw wouldn't have gone as far as it did!"

Only then did Bazza realise that Trev was placing the last marker on a spot way beyond his own.

"And the Angels FC long throw-in specialist is – Lulu!"

Bazza had annoyed her so much that her final murderous throw-in had won the competition!

"I think you owe me five pounds," smiled Lulu, holding her hand out beneath his nose.

What a disaster! He'd lost his Twister
Thompson winnings already!

That evening, Bazza sat and brooded.
Bets were good if you won. Losing a bet,
though, was horrible. And losing a bet
to a girl with pigtails was just about as
horrible as it could get.

So, either he'd have to stop betting – or
make sure he won next time. Bazza made his
decision with a grim determination. He was
going to win next time. And to repair his
injured pride, next time simply had to be a bet
to recover his five pounds from Lulu Squibb.

It was just a case of working out how to
get her to walk into another, superior, trap…

3

Injury Time

When Bazza arrived at school on Wednesday morning, Twister Thompson was standing glumly by the gates, a crisp five pound note between his fingers.

"Make the most of it," scowled Twister, handing the money to Bazza, "because you won't be keeping it for long."

"You never spoke a truer word, Twister!" said Lulu, plucking the note straight from Bazza's fingers. "A pleasure to do business with you, Bazza!"

"You – you didn't lose
a bet to *her*?" asked Twister
as Lulu skipped away with
the money.

Bazza nodded glumly. "She won't
have it long. I'm going to win it back."

"How?" asked Twister.

"Er…I haven't worked that out, yet."

Twister looked thoughtful. Wickedly
thoughtful. "Now I might just be able to
help you there," he said slowly.

"Oh, yeah?" Bazza wasn't sure he could
trust Twister Thompson any further than he
could throw him, with or without a bad
arm. But if it helped recover that money it
would be worth the risk. "How?"

"By talking her into having another bet. When you win that five pounds back you can give it to me for helping. Then I won't have lost any money."

And I'll have shown Lulu Squibb who's got the superior talent, thought Bazza. He drew Twister to one side so that they couldn't be overheard.

"So what's your idea? It had better be good. I thought I was going to win my bet with her last time!"

Twister gave a little chuckle. "Ah, but last time you didn't have me to help you, Bazza. The bet I'm thinking about now is a sure-fire certainty!"

"A certainty, eh?" Bazza had to hear more about that. "What is it?"

"You bet Lulu Squibb that I'll score a goal next Saturday."

It didn't sound like a certainty to Bazza. "Who are Maddox Rebels playing?" he asked.

"Maddox Rebels," said Twister carefully, "are playing Totton Tykes."

Now that *was* a certainty! "We beat Totton Tykes 12–0!" cried Bazza. "We all banged in a goal! Well, everybody except Tarlock, and he only missed out because he didn't want to score."

"Why not?"

"That's another story,"[2] said Bazza. "The point is, you are bound to score a goal if you're playing Totton Tykes."

Even as he said it, Bazza saw the huge flaw in the plan. "But Lulu will think just the same, won't she? So why would she be

[2] See *Goal Greedy*

daft enough to bet me that you won't score?"

Twister tapped the side of his nose and winked. "Because I'll pretend to be injured. She'll think I'm not even playing!"

"Pretend to be injured? Forget it!" Bazza started to walk away. "That's the trick I worked on her before.

She won't fall for it again!"

"Oh yes she will," said Twister, hurrying to his side. "'Cos she's going to see me get injured with her very own eyes…"

⚽ ⚽ ⚽

The trap was set for next day, at going-home time. Racing out quickly, Bazza and Twister waited near the bike sheds until they saw

Lulu coming their way. Then, dropping a tennis ball on to the ground, Twister began dribbling it around.

"Come on then, Wattso," he shouted, loud enough for Lulu to hear. "You can't be lucky all the time. Let's see you take the ball off me now!"

Seeing Lulu look their way, Bazza cried, "No problem, Twister! The bike sheds are the goal. If you can score, I'm a baby baboon!"

Dribbling the tennis ball close, Twister hissed, "Right, she's seen us. Time for phase two!"

"Phase two it is," Bazza hissed back. "Go for it."

Shimmying and turning, Twister began racing towards the bike sheds. In front of him, Bazza ran backwards as though waiting for his moment to tackle.

The plan was that Twister wouldn't try
to go past him until they were within
touching distance of the bike sheds. Then
Bazza would pretend to tackle him, after
which Twister would pretend to go flying
into the bikes and come out pretending to
have hurt his leg.

So the last thing Bazza expected was for
Twister to forget his own plan and barge
into him while there was still a good couple
of metres to go. Thrown off balance, Bazza
clattered backwards into a mountain bike
while, with a graceful dive, Twister dropped
carefully to the ground.

"Ooooohhhhhh!" groaned Bazza.

"Aaaagggghhhh!" yelled Twister.

By the time Bazza
had pulled himself free
and Twister was back
on his feet, Lulu had
arrived on the scene.

"Are you two all
right?" she asked.

Twister made a face.
"Not sure," he winced.
"I think I may have
hurt my ankle. I'll
have to see how
it is tomorrow."

"What about you?"
Lulu asked Bazza as
Twister limped away.

"You're not going
to believe this," said
Bazza, gritting his
teeth. "I've hurt
my wrist!"

Lulu turned on her heel. "You're absolutely right, Bazza. I'm *not* going to believe it!"

Bazza tucked his hand inside his jacket to try to ease the pain. Lulu believing *him* didn't matter so much. The really important question was: would she believe *Twister*?

4

You Twister!

"What do you reckon?" Twister asked Bazza
next morning. They were behind the bike sheds
again, waiting for Lulu to arrive.

Bazza looked Twister up and down. He'd
done a convincing job, there was no doubt about
that. Not only had he limped in on a pair of
crutches wearing an outsized trainer on his right
foot, but somehow he'd managed to change his
ankle into one shaped more like a melon.

"How did you get it to look like that?"
asked Bazza.

"Four pairs of socks," said Twister,
"and a couple of lumps of bath sponge. The
trainer belongs to me big brother – and the
crutches were in the cupboard under the
stairs from when me dad stuck a garden
fork through his foot while he was digging
the garden!"

"Well it would have fooled me. But will it
fool Lulu?"

Twister glanced out towards the front gate. "We'll soon find out. Here she comes!"

Bazza watched as Twister limped away across the playground looking more like Long John Silver than a wicked winger.

He saw Twister nod at Lulu.

He saw Lulu gape at him open-mouthed, point at his ankle, and exchange a few words.

Then, the moment she headed off into school, Bazza raced round the back way and in through a side entrance so that he couldn't help bumping into her as she walked down the corridor towards him.

"Morning, Lulu!" he said brightly.

Lulu didn't waste words. "Have you seen Twister Thompson?"

"No. Why, still sulking after that pitiful attempt to dribble round me with his tennis ball, is he?"

"No, he's—"

Bazza quickly interrupted her. "Looking chirpy? I'm not surprised. He must be relieved he's not facing me again. He knows he'll probably bang in a couple of goals this week."

"No he won't," said Lulu, starting to go pink.

"Lulu, Lulu," said Bazza, shaking his head as though he was talking to a twit. "Face facts. I am a star. He'll never score against me. But against anybody else he's bound to get at least one."

Lulu clenched her fists and tried once more. "Listen, you big banana, I'm telling

you Twister Thompson won't score a goal
this weekend because—"

"Because you know nothing about
marking wickedly tricky wingers!" said
Bazza, encouraged by how annoyed Lulu
had already become. "Unlike me, the best
defender in Defender-land, who knows
everything there is to know about
wickedly tricky wingers. And I bet you
that Twister Thompson *does* score
a goal tomorrow!"

It was the last straw.
"Right," snarled Lulu,
"how much?"

"Five pounds,"
replied Bazza instantly.

"Done!" said Lulu.
"I bet you he *won't* score
tomorrow."
She grabbed Bazza's hand
and shook it to confirm the bet.

"Ouch!" squawked Bazza, wincing as a sharp jab of pain shot up his wrist.

"And stop pretending you've hurt your wrist," snapped Lulu. "Go and have a look at Twister's ankle. That's a real injury!"

Bazza put on his best astonished look. "Twister? Injured ankle?"

"Twister's twisted it!" crowed Lulu. "He was hobbling on crutches when I saw him. So there you go, Mr Big Banana Know-It-All. Even a super whizz-bang tip-top star like you can't score a goal if you're not playing. And by the look of that ankle, Twister won't be playing tomorrow!"

⚽   ⚽   ⚽

"It worked a treat!" laughed Bazza when he met Twister after school. "She fell for it completely!"

Twister smiled. "So she's bet you that I won't score a goal tomorrow, and you've bet her I will. Right?"

172

"Right!" grinned Bazza. "And with Maddox Rebels playing against Totton Tykes' leaky old defence you can't fail to score at least one – and I can't lose!"

Twister's smile took a wicked twist. "Maddox Rebels? Oh, silly me. I clean forgot to tell you. I'm not playing for them any more."

"Wha– wha–" burbled Bazza. "Wha– what do you mean?"

"I mean, Bazza the Bighead," said Twister triumphantly, "I've signed on with another team. Welby Wolves!"

"Welby Wolves? But – the Angels are playing Welby Wolves tomorrow! So – I'll be marking you again."

"Yeah," said Twister, frowning. "I was hoping to injure a bit more than your arm when we played our tackling trick on little Squibbo. I was hoping to put you out of the game. Still it doesn't matter now. Having you up against me will make it that much more fun."

"No it won't," snarled Bazza. "An injured arm won't stop me marking you out of the game." Twister slung his crutches over his shoulder and gave a little dance of joy.

"Ah, but you can't do that, can you? 'Cos if you don't let me score in the game tomorrow..."

Bazza closed his eyes in despair. "I'll lose my bet," he groaned.

5

The Gambler's Last Throw

Bazza was well and truly trapped. If he didn't want to lose his bet, he'd have to risk the Angels losing the match by going easy on Twister and allowing him to score a goal. But if he did that, Lulu would be gunning for him – as she quickly made clear as the teams ran out.

"It's Twister!" cried Lulu, seeing the winger sprint across the pitch in his new colours. "He's playing! For Welby Wolves!"

"Yeah," said Bazza gloomily. "Looks like he made a miracle recovery."

Lulu eyed him suspiciously. "Well just make sure there isn't another miracle, and he scores a goal against the best defender in Defender-land."

"He might," said Bazza. "These things happen."

Standing on tiptoe, Lulu put her fist against Bazza's nose. "He'd better not," she said menacingly. "Because if you let him score to make me lose that bet, then the next thing you'll find happening will be me cleaning my football boots on your shorts – while you're still wearing them!"

And so, not daring to do otherwise, Bazza played his usual game and hardly gave Twister a kick throughout the whole of the first half.

"Silly," hissed the winger as the whistle blew for the half-time break with the score at 0–0. "Very silly. You won't win the money that way. Still, let's hope you see sense in the second half."

"Very good, Bazza," hissed Lulu, "let's hope you see sense in the second half as well."

Bazza's heart fell. Should he resign himself to losing the bet? Or should he give Twister a goal on a plate and resign himself to being chewed into bits by Lulu the Lioness? Was there any way out of this mess?

If there was, Bazza couldn't see it.

Glumly, he listened to Trev giving his half-time pep talk.

"Their defence is playing well," the Angels coach was saying. "So we're going to have to try to do something from set pieces – free kicks, corners – and don't forget our long throw-in tactic. Bazza, if we get one near their penalty area you move up to join the attack. See if you can get on the end of one of Lulu's long throws. Got that?"

Bazza nodded furiously. He'd got it, all right. It was the perfect excuse. He couldn't be in two places at once. So he'd join the attack at every opportunity. If he could score a few goals himself, then it wouldn't matter if the Wolves got one as a consolation. And if it just happened to be Twister who scored because Bazza wasn't marking him…well, it wouldn't be his fault, would it? Lulu would have to accept that he'd only been obeying Trev's orders!

With renewed hope, Bazza launched himself forward as soon as the match restarted. Charging between two Wolves defenders, he screamed for a pass. Mick Ryall played it through as Bazza surged towards the penalty box – only to find himself beaten to it by the Wolves goalkeeper kicking it into touch.

"Lulu! Up you go, Throw-in Champ!" yelled Lennie Gould.

Lulu sprinted forward to take the throw, while Bazza ran into the goal mouth to join the cluster of Angels players waiting for the ball to arrive.

Except that – it didn't. Even though Lulu ran in and heaved with all her might, her throw carried no further than the edge of the goal area and was easily cleared.

The same thing happened ten minutes later, and again not long after that. Lulu seemed to have completely lost her throw-in power. They were causing no danger at all.

With five minutes left and the score still 0–0, the Angels won yet another throw. Bazza knew it was his last chance. If Twister was going to have time to hit a consolation goal, the Angels had got to score a couple themselves – and pretty soon.

Dashing across to the touchline, Bazza snatched up the ball.

"Hey! I take the throws!" said Lulu, scuttling up.

"Not this one, you don't," said Bazza, taking a couple of steps back. In he ran, pulled his arms back over his head, yanked them forward again – and yelled!

"Owwwww!!"

In the heat of the moment he'd forgotten about his injured wrist. As the pain shot up his arm he dropped the ball – straight at the feet of a Wolves defender, who switched it quickly up the line to Twister Thompson!

"Go, Twister!" screamed the Wolves players.

It seemed as if he must score. With most of the Angels defenders up with the attack, he had a clear run on goal. But, as Kirsten Browne edged out to meet him, a sudden, whirling, screeching Angels-shirted blur caught him up and hammered the ball into touch. Lulu!

"You big cheating banana!" she snarled at Bazza as he struggled back. "You threw that to him on purpose! You wait till the game's over! I'm going to—"

She didn't finish. The throw had been taken, Tarlock Bhasin had won the ball, slid it through to Rhoda O'Neill, and the Angels were on the attack again. With a surging run, Rhoda was closing in on the Wolves goal when she too was stopped by a good tackle and the ball put out for another Angels throw.

"Mine!" roared Lulu, defying Bazza to argue.

Bazza didn't. Knowing that time had almost run out, he trudged forward yet again. There was no hope now. He'd lost the bet. At least if he helped Angels win the match it might make him feel a bit better about things.

The Wolves captain saw him coming. "Twister!" he yelled, pointing at Bazza. "Mark him!"

What a disaster! Instead of him helping Twister score, the game was going to end with Twister trying to stop Bazza!

Or was it? As the Wolves winger tailed him into the goal area, Bazza had an idea. Could it work?

He glanced out to the touchline. It could if Lulu managed to produce a throw-in like she had in the competition. So far today, though, she'd come nowhere near it. Why not?

Because she wasn't annoyed enough, of course! On Tuesday night he'd got her so wound up she could have thrown *him* into the penalty area! But was her temper rising now?

She certainly wasn't calm, that was for sure. As she got ready to take her throw-in,

Bazza could see from the look on her face that she was still steamed up at what she thought was his attempt at cheating.

So…maybe if he irritated her just a little bit more…

"Lulu!" bawled Bazza. "Try and get it past the end of your nose this time, eh?"

From out on the touchline Lulu glared daggers at him. "WHAT?!"

"You heard! Try harder! A worm with a walking stick could manage a longer throw-in than you!"

Even as he said it, Bazza edged back towards the Wolves goal. From right behind him came the voice of Twister Thompson. "She's not happy with you, Bazza. Not happy at all."

He was right. Lulu was steaming up to take the throw as if she was about to burst! "Yaaaaaahhhhhh!!!" she howled, firing the ball straight at Bazza's head just as she had in the competition.

Perfect! Waiting until the rocketing ball was almost on him, Bazza suddenly dived out of the way – so that it smacked the astonished Twister on the head and shot into the roof of the Wolves net for an own goal!

"Yes!" screamed Bazza. "You've scored, Twister! Angels win the match – and I win the bet!!"

After the whistle had gone to give the Angels
a 1–0 win, Bazza lost no time in seeking out
Lulu in the changing rooms.

She'd seen him coming and had produced
the five pound note before he could say
a word. "All right, I know what you want.
Here it is."

Bazza shook his head. "No, that's not what
I want, Lulu. I want to say sorry. Twister
nearly made a fool of both of us, and it was
all my fault. You keep the money."

"Not likely," said Lulu, breaking into the
most enormous grin. "It was worth a fiver
just to see my throw hit Twister on
the bonce!"

"Let's share it then."

Lulu thrust the money into Bazza's fingers. "No. You have it. You won the bet."

"A bet?" said Trev, coming between them. His voice was icy. "Bazza, do I have to remind you of the Angels code? 'Angels on and off the pitch!' And you can take it from me that angels do not bet!"

Bazza nodded. "I know, Trev. And don't worry, I've learnt my lesson. I've given it up."

"Are you sure, Bazza?"

"Positive, Trev. I'll never bet again!"

"That's easier said than done," said Trev. "I think you will do it again."

"I won't!" cried Bazza, annoyed.

Trev shook his head seriously. He sucked his teeth. "I bet you do," he said solemnly.

"I bet you five pounds I don't!" shouted Bazza.

Even as Bazza realised what he'd said, Trev was whipping the five pound note from his fingers.

"I win!" said Trev. "And let that be a lesson to you, Bazza. Betting's a mug's game."

"What are you going to spend your winnings on, Trev?" laughed Lulu.

"I'm going to put it into club funds," said Trev. "That way it won't be wasted – you can bet on that!"